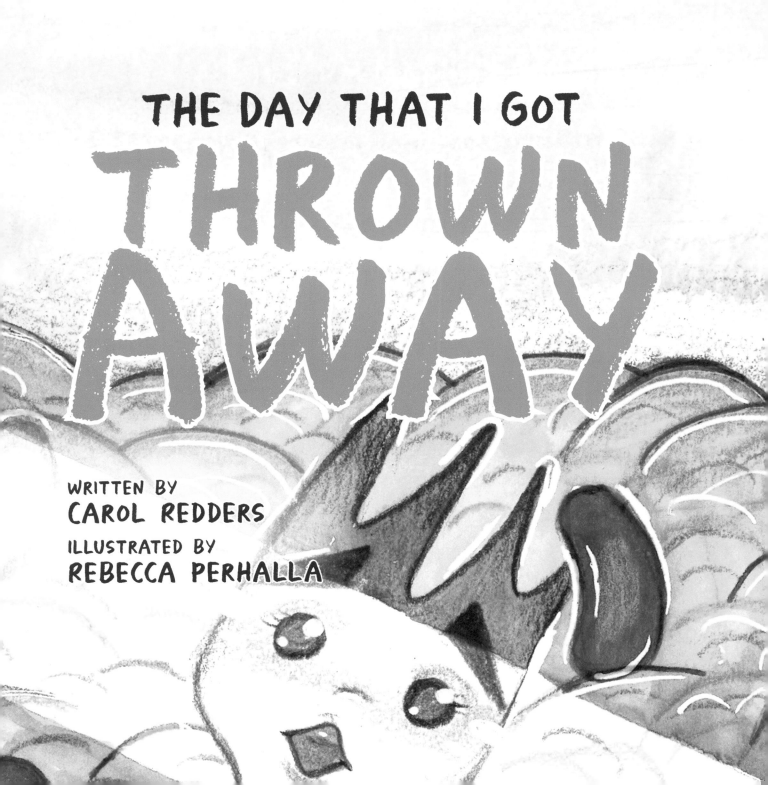

THE DAY THAT I GOT
THROWN
AWAY

WRITTEN BY
CAROL REDDERS

ILLUSTRATED BY
REBECCA PERHALLA

Published by Orange Hat Publishing 2019
ISBN 978-1-64538-076-4

For information, please contact:

Orange Hat Publishing
www.orangehatpublishing.com
Waukesha, WI

Today started like a normal day.
I woke up to great smells floating my way
in the school kitchen where I lay.

THE DAY THAT I GOT THROWN AWAY.

Then at the same time as every other day,
I felt myself moving, starting to sway.
The worker arrived to take me where
the children would pick up their silverware.

Waiting to be picked and placed on a tray,
I wondered, "Who would choose me that day
to carry food into their mouth?
I am important, there is no doubt!"

Then I felt a warm soft grip;
inside my heart, I felt a flip.
All through lunch I was handled with care,
holding food in my prongs, both beans and pears.

I listened to chatter all around.
Voices of children, there's no better sound!
Then came clapping and a big, strong voice
quieting the children above all the noise.

"Children, it's time to finish your lunch.
Let me hear you crunch and munch!
Clean up and close your milk carton too.
Don't leave any garbage. Chew, chew, chew!"

"The quietest table is first to go.
One at a time, let's walk in a row.
Carrying your tray with both of your hands,
please walk slowly to the garbage cans."

The children stood up and started to walk.
Balancing their trays, quietly they talked.
They stopped first to put their silverware away
to soak in a bucket until the end of the day.

Then the child whose tray I was on
jumped up from her seat and hurried along.
Suddenly, I smelled something stinky and strong.
Then I knew something was terribly wrong!

I found myself flying into the air.
Would anyone notice or even care?
I landed beside a bean and a pear.
I wanted to cry out, but did I dare?

There wasn't going to be much time.
I wasn't okay! I wasn't fine!
I wanted to live another day.

THE DAY THAT I GOT THROWN AWAY.

So I took a deep breath and I shouted out,
"Someone, please help me out!"
I didn't know if anyone would hear,
but then I heard the worker's voice near.

"I hear something. Do you hear it too?
Someone is crying. What should we do?"
Then I saw the most beautiful sight,
as the worker's hand came through the light.

As her hand reached in and picked me out,
I was so happy, I wanted to shout!
Not wanting to scare the children away,
I decided it best, not to yell, hooray!

As I arose from the garbage can,
I saw my hero and felt her soft hand.
She winked as she looked over at me,
and said she heard my heart-felt plea.

Then the happiest words did I hear,
as she told the children that were near,
"Be careful when you empty your trays.
We reuse silverware here each day!"

"For tomorrow is another day,
you will pick silverware for your tray.
Let's learn a lesson from this mistake.
Let's save the silverware for goodness sake!"

Then I was placed in the bucket to soak.
I would live another day. I had hope!
I learned how important I am that day.

THE DAY THAT I GOT THROWN AWAY.

DISCUSSION QUESTIONS

1. Has anyone ever felt like the fork in this story (invisible, ignored, lonely, not important, thrown away, etc.)?

2. Who are people in this school, or outside of school, who you can talk to when you feel like this?

3. What can you do if you see a classmate who looks like they are lonely or ignored?

4. What are some ways you can show responsibility and respect in the lunchroom?

AUTHOR'S NOTE

For anyone who has ever felt like the fork in this story (invisible, not important, or thrown away), I want you to know that:

YOU are **NOT** invisible
You **ARE** Important
YOU MATTER

I know what it's like to feel invisible, like I'm not important, like I don't matter. I also know what it feels like to be thrown away. You are not alone!

If you have ever felt any of these strong emotions, I want you to know that I am sorry and it is not your fault.

I also want you to know that there is HOPE. Even though many of us have experienced these feelings from past hardships or trauma, we can heal. We can overcome. I am living proof. I am an overcomer! You can be an overcomer too!

CPSIA information can be obtained
at www.ICGtesting.com
Printed in the USA
BVHW020936251019
561432BV00004B/2/P